ST. DANIEL
FAITH FORMATION OFFICE
7010 VALLEY PARK DR.
CLARKSTON, MI 48346

THE STRAY

Story by Gerard A. Pottebaum
Art by Mary Jo Scandin

DEDICATIONS

To Julie, Cecilia, David, John
and all of my grandchildren
in celebration of finding one another.
GAP

To my children, Corey, Gigi, and Angela
with fond zoo memories.
MJS

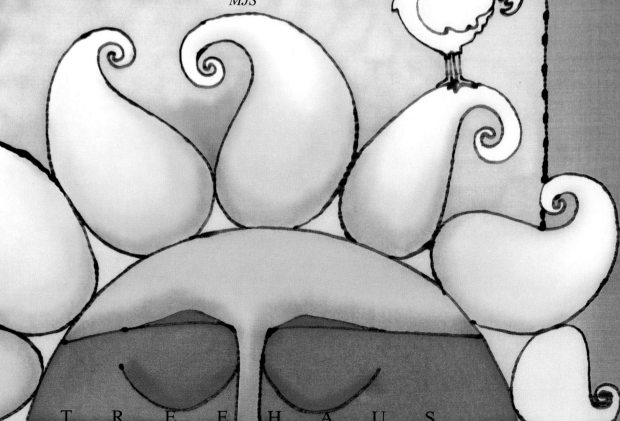

T R E E H A U S

TREEHAUS COMMUNICATIONS, INC. • P. O. BOX 249 • LOVELAND, OHIO 45140-0249

One magnolia morning
a friend of the poor
took ten children
to the city zoo.

ISBN 1-886510-54-7 Illustrations and text © 2001 by Treehaus Communications, Inc. Loveland, Ohio 45140-0249.

They broke loose
like squirrels uncaged
in a walnut grove.

They skipped and scampered to see the monkeys swinging from bar to branch.

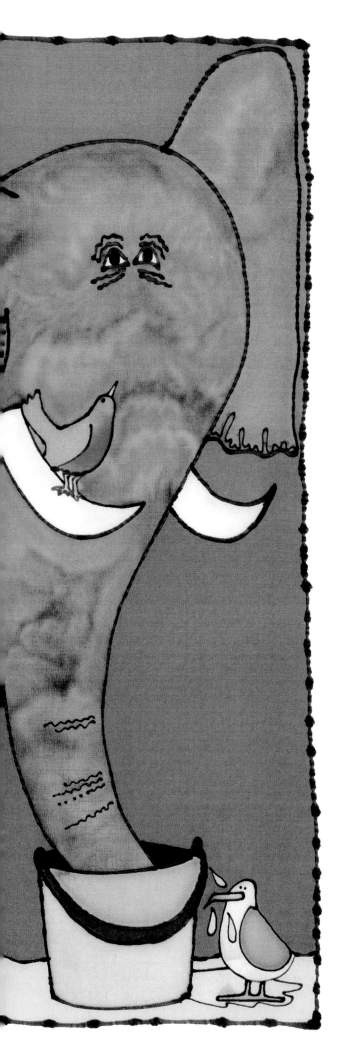

They wondered
about the elephant
drinking through its nose.
Whenever they tried it,
they would choke.

They tried to count the spots on the leopards.

But there were so many, they could not keep track of the
spots they had counted and those they had missed.

When they saw the zebras, they tried to count their stripes.
But after they finished, they were confused again.

Some had counted black stripes. Others had counted white stripes.
And still others had counted both the white and the black stripes.

When time came to go home, they gathered at the bus and agreed to count noses to make sure that no one would be left behind.

But when they finished counting,
their happy faces turned sad.
They could count only nine
when they knew there should be ten.

Someone was missing.

Someone was lost.

"Wait here until I come back," their friend said and,

in a big hurry, left the nine who were safe to find the one who was lost.

Their friend searched
the pathways and cages,
around the benches and
behind the bushes . . .

. . . until at last their friend spotted the lost child
crying dinosaur tears under a chestnut tree.

Their friend ran to the child with a warm hug . . .

. . . and carried the child back to the ringing cheers
of the nine who were waiting.

"This really is something to shout about," their friend said.

Then, to everyone's surprise, their friend bought them cones of their favorite flavors!

They were happier
over the one
who was found
than over the nine
who were never lost.

A PARABLE.